World of Reading

LEVEL 3

PERRY SPEAKS!

Adapted by Ellie O'Ryan
Based on the series created by Dan Povenmire & Jeff "Swampy" Marsh

ABDO
Spotlight

DISNEY PRESS
New York

WWW.ABDOPUBLISHING.COM

Reinforced library bound edition published in 2015 by Spotlight, a division of ABDO
PO Box 398166, Minneapolis, Minnesota 55439. Spotlight produces high-quality
reinforced library bound editions for schools and libraries. Published by Disney Press,
an imprint of Disney Book Group.

Printed in the United States of America, North Mankato, Minnesota.
052014
072014

 DISNEP PRESS   ♻ THIS BOOK CONTAINS
RECYCLED MATERIALS

LIBRARY OF CONGRESS CATALOGING-IN-PUBLICATION DATA

This title was previously cataloged with the following information:

O'Ryan, Ellie.
 Phineas and Ferb: Perry speaks!/ adapted by Ellie O'Ryan.
  p. cm. -- (World of reading. Level 3)
Summary: Phineas and Ferb build a "Perry translator" so they can finally understand
what Perry the Platypus is saying.
1. Stepbrothers--Juvenile fiction. 2. Platypus--Juvenile fiction. I. Marsh, Jeff, 1960- II.
Povenmire, Dan. III. Disney Enterprises (1996-) IV. Phineas and Ferb (Television
program) V. Title. VI. Series.
PZ7.O78417Pe 2012
[E]--dc23

2011943366

978-1-61479-270-3 (Reinforced Library Bound Edition)

Spotlight
A Division of ABDO
www.abdopublishing.com

A Note to Parents

Your child is beginning the lifelong adventure of reading! And with the **World of Reading** program, you can be sure that he or she is receiving the encouragement needed to become a confident, independent reader. This program is specially designed to encourage your child to enjoy reading at every level by combining exciting, easy-to-read stories featuring favorite characters with colorful art that brings the magic to life.

The **World of Reading** program is divided into four levels so that children at any stage can enjoy a successful reading experience:

Reader-in-Training
Pre-K–Kindergarten
Picture reading and word repetition for children who are getting ready to read.

Beginner Reader
Pre-K–Grade 1
Simple stories and easy-to-sound-out words for children who are just learning to read.

Junior Reader
Kindergarten–Grade 2
Slightly longer stories and more varied sentences perfect for children who are reading with the help of a parent.

Super Reader
Grade 1–Grade 3
Encourages independent reading with rich story lines and wide vocabulary that's just right for children who are reading on their own.

Learning to read is a once-in-a-lifetime adventure, and with **World of Reading**, the journey is just beginning!

One summer day, Phineas and Ferb were in the backyard. Their pet platypus, Perry, was there, too.

"What to do, what to do, what to do today," Phineas said. "Any ideas, Ferb?"

Ferb just shrugged.

"How about you, Perry?" Phineas asked. "Bursting with any plans?"

Perry made his chittering noise.

"I wonder what that means," Phineas said. Then he had an idea. "Ferb, let's build a Perry translator!"

The boys went right to work. They built a huge machine. It was covered with switches, buttons, and dials. It even had a microphone and a giant speaker.

"Now all we need is our subject," said Phineas. "Where's Perry?"

The brothers looked to the left. They looked to the right. They looked up and down. But Perry had disappeared!

Phineas and Ferb didn't know
that their pet was actually a secret
agent. And he was on his way to an
important meeting with his boss,
Major Monogram!

Perry put on his hat to transform
into Agent P. Then he used a remote
control to enter his hidden lair.

Agent P watched Major Monogram on a large computer screen. But the lights kept blinking on and off.

"Sorry about the lights," the major said. "We're using a new energy source and haven't quite got it working smoothly yet."

Major Monogram held up a piece
of paper. It was covered in black ink.

"We're saving paper by printing on
the same piece over and over again,"
he said. "For the life of me, I can't
make this out. Well, I'm sure it says
something about Doofenshmirtz. Go
get him!"

After Agent P left, Major Monogram went to check on the new energy source. It was Carl the intern. He was pedaling an exercise bike to power the lights!

"Carl, pedal faster!" Major Monogram ordered. "I've got to check my e-mail."

Agent P ran through the backyard.
He needed to find his enemy, Dr.
Doofenshmirtz. But before he could
sneak by, Phineas spotted him.

"Oh, there you are!" Phineas said.
He took the platypus over to the animal
translator. "It's time to hear what's on
your mind."

Just as Perry was about to speak, Isabella came into the yard.

"What'cha doin'?" she asked.

"Ferb and I have invented a Perry translator," Phineas replied.

"That's great!" Isabella said. "But don't you need Perry to be here for it to work?"

Phineas turned around. The platypus had disappeared again!

Just then, the friends heard a small,
squeaky voice behind them.

"I sure love worms!" it said. "Big, fat,
juicy worms! Got to find them. Got to
eat them!"

The friends turned around and saw that a bird had landed on the animal translator's microphone. Every time the bird chirped, the machine translated what it said!

Phineas was thrilled. The invention really worked!

Phineas decided to see if the machine worked on other animals, too.

"How about you?" he asked a squirrel. "Do you understand me?"

"Oh, I do!" the squirrel replied. "Do you have any nuts for me?"

"That's so cute!" cried Isabella. "Do you think it would work on my dog, Pinky?"

"It couldn't hurt to try," Phineas said. "With a device like this, all animals can finally say what's on their minds!"

The bird overheard what Phineas said. It went to tell some pigeons.

The pigeons told a dog.

The dog told a bunch of cats.
Soon, all the animals in Danville
were on their way to Phineas and Ferb's
backyard!

Each animal used the machine to tell
Phineas about its problems.

A chubby orange cat meowed into
the microphone. It wanted its owners to
give it more food.

"I see what you're saying," Phineas
said. "But they're giving you twelve
cans a day. Technically, you're not
underfed."

Next, a black dog barked into the translator.

"Oh, yeah," Phineas said, nodding. "I've been getting a lot of complaints about the vacuum. Just let it out."

Meanwhile, across town, Agent P
was searching for Dr. Doofenshmirtz.
He found the evil doctor deep in the
forest. The platypus was just about to
sneak up on him when . . .

Thwack!

A giant cage landed right on top of
Agent P.

"Ha, ha!" Dr. Doofenshmirtz laughed.
"You like my new cage? I got it from a
secondhand shark-supply store. It was
half off because something bit half of
it off!"

Now that Agent P was trapped,
Dr. Doofenshmirtz told the platypus all
about his evil plan.

"With this remote, I will open the
Danville Dam, flooding all the streets,"
Dr. Doofenshmirtz said. "But how will
people get around?"

"They will have to buy my latest invention!" he cried. "It's like a car, but it can drive on water. Behold!"

He yanked a sheet off a large object next to him. There was a boat under it. "I call it the Buoyancy Operated Aquatic Transport, or Bo-At, for short," he said. "Everyone will want one!"

Back at home, Phineas and Ferb's older sister, Candace, was worried.

Her crush, Jeremy, hadn't called in four days. "I'm not expecting Prince Charming to bring me a glass slipper," she said. "But a phone call would be nice."

Just then, Candace's phone beeped. It was Jeremy! He asked if she wanted to play video games with him.

Knock-knock-knock!

"Hold on, Candace," Jeremy said into the phone. "Someone's at the door."

When Jeremy opened it, Candace was standing there! She had run all the way from her house.

"So, video games?" she asked.

Candace and Jeremy started playing a game. Suddenly, a tiny poodle jumped up on the couch. It belonged to Jeremy's little sister, Suzie.

The dog growled at Candace.

Then it peed on her shoe!

Candace tried to dry her shoe with some paper towels. "I can't believe this!" she grumbled.

But Suzie's dog still wanted to bother her. It ran off with her shoe!

"Hey!" Candace cried. She chased the dog into the bathroom. It held her shoe over the toilet.

"Don't even think about it!" Candace warned.

Candace tried to flush the paper towels she had used to dry her shoe down the toilet. But Suzie's dog dropped the shoe in, too. The toilet clogged up!

"No, no, no!" Candace cried. Paper towels and toilet water exploded all over the bathroom. Candace's shoe flew out, too.

Candace didn't want Jeremy to see her covered in toilet water. She ran home, leaving her soggy shoe behind.

Meanwhile, in the backyard, Isabella gave Phineas an update.

"We've got seventy-eight complaints about food quantity," she said. "And forty-two requests for belly rubs."

One of the Fireside Girls joined them. "The Jones' hamster says it's

going to lose it if someone doesn't oil the wheel in its cage," she said.

"So what are we supposed to do with this information?" Isabella asked.

"Let's tell all the owners what their pets want!" Phineas exclaimed.

Just then, Candace got home. She was in a really bad mood. "What is going on here?" she yelled.

"We made an animal translator," Phineas explained.

Candace groaned. "I have had it with stupid animals today!" she shouted.

The animals didn't like what Candace said. A big dog barked into the microphone.

"Get her!" the machine translated.

The animals chased Candace!

Back in the forest, Dr. Doofenshmirtz pushed the button on his remote control.

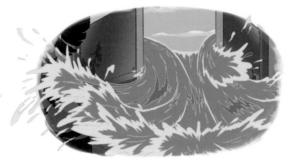

The Danville Dam opened. Water flooded out.

The Bo-At started to float!

Luckily, the water also knocked over Agent P's cage. The platypus swam to safety and jumped onto the Bo-At.

"Perry the Platypus!" the evil doctor exclaimed. "I always forget that you are a semi-aquatic mammal."

Across town, the animals chased
Candace through the city . . .

. . . and into the forest!

Suddenly, the river Dr. Doofenshmirtz
had released from the dam washed over
everything. It swept the animals up into
the Bo-At!

The water rushed toward downtown Danville. Agent P knew that he didn't have much time. He dived off the Bo-At and swam as fast as he could to a high wall with a wheel on it.

"Don't open that!" the doctor cried.

Agent P turned the wheel. A moat
around Danville opened just in time.
All the water flowed around the city.
Danville was saved!

Now that Dr. Doofenshmirtz's evil plan had been stopped, Perry sneaked back home. When Phineas, Ferb, and Isabella returned to the yard, Perry was waiting for them.

Candace hurried home, too. She dragged her mom into the backyard.

"Mom, come on!" she cried. "You've got to see this!"

If nothing else, Candace wanted to bust her brothers!

Phineas set up the microphone in front of Perry. "Okay," he said. "We've been waiting all day for this."

Perry made his chittering noise. Everyone waited. Then . . .

Brbrbrbrbrbr!

The animal translator played the chittering noise right back!

"Oh, well," Phineas said. "I guess it doesn't mean anything."

"Aww," Mom said. "You know he's saying, 'You guys are the best!' Now come inside for some lemonade."

Candace couldn't believe it. Her brothers had gotten away without being busted again!

Just then, Jeremy walked up. "Hey, Candace!" he called. "I brought your shoe. I washed it. Here, allow me."

Jeremy slipped the shoe onto Candace's foot. She felt just like a princess—and fainted!

"Candace? You okay?" Jeremy asked.

"Enchanted!" she replied.